to Sarah

from Sandy, Doug, Simone + Michelle
        Ronco

Dec. 1978

to Sarah

from Sandy, Doug, Simone + Michelle

Aunt Louisa's
Rip Van Winkle

Aunt Louisa's Rip Van Winkle

LOUISA PENN WILLINGTON

Hart Publishing Company, Inc. New York City

COPYRIGHT © 1977, HART PUBLISHING COMPANY, INC.
NEW YORK, NEW YORK 10012

ISBN NO. 08055-0357-9
LIBRARY OF CONGRESS CATALOG CARD NO. 77-79198

MANUFACTURED IN THE UNITED STATES OF AMERICA

Aunt Louisa's
Rip Van Winkle

RIP VAN WINKLE

NEAR to the town, in a cottage small,
Lived RIP VAN WINKLE, known to all
As a harmless, drinking, shiftless lout,
Who never would work, but roamed about,
Always ready with jest and song—
Idling, tippling all day long.

"Shame on you—Rip!" cried the scolding fraus;
And old men muttered and knit their brows.
Not so with the boys, for they would shout,
And follow their hero, Rip, about,
Early or late—it was all the same,
They gave him a place in every game.

At ball he was ready to throw or catch;
At marbles, too, he was quite their match;

And many an urchin's
    face grew bright
When Rip took hold
    of his twine and kite.

And so he frittered the time away—
"Good-natured enough," they all would say.
But the village parson heaved a sigh
As Rip, in his cups, went reeling by,
With a silly and a drunken leer—
His good dog Wolfie always near.

Rip was fond of his rod and line,
And many a time, when the day was fine,
He would wander out to some neighb'ring stream,
And there, with his dog, would sit and dream;
Hour after hour, would he dozing wait,
And woe to the fish that touched his bait.

But the stream of his life ran sometimes rough,

And his good wife gave him many a cuff,

For she was never a gentle dame,

And Rip was a drunkard, and much to blame.

But little did Rip Van Winkle care

For his wife or his home—he was seldom there—

But tried in his cups his cares to drown;

His scolding wife, with her threat'ning frown,

At his cottage-door he was sure to see—

"Ah! this," said Rip,

"is no place for me."

So down to the tavern to drink his rum,

And waste his time with some red-nosed chum,

He was sure to go; for he knew that there

He would find a glass and a vacant chair,

And jolly fellows, who liked his fun,

And the tales he told of his dog and gun.

But his was still but a sorry life,
For, sot as he was, he loved his wife;
But he would tipple both day and night,
And she would scold him with all her might.
Thus Rip Van Winkle had many a grief,
And up 'mongst the mountains sought relief.

For lowering clouds or a burning sun
He cared but little; his dog and gun
Were his friends, he knew; while they were near
He roamed the forests, and felt no fear.

If tired at last, and a seat he took,
And his dog came up with a hungry look,
He had always a crust or bone to spare,
And Wolfie was certain to get his share.

And then if a squirrel chanced to stray
In range of his gun, he would blaze away,
And he held it too with a steady aim—
Rip never was known to miss his game.

But over his ills he would sometimes brood,
And scale the peaks in a gloomy mood;
And once he had climbed to a dizzy height,
When the sun went down, and the shades of night
Came up from the vale, and the pine-trees tall,
And the old gray rocks, and the waterfall
Grew dusky and dim and faded away,
Till night, like a pall, on the mountain lay.

Full many a mile he had strayed that day,
And up in the mountains had lost his way;
And there he must stay through the gloomy night,
And shiver and wait for the morning light.

He thought of the stories, strange and old,
Which the graybeards down in the village told;
"And what," said he, "if the tale were true
I have heard so oft of a phantom crew
Who up in the Catskills, all night long,
Frolic and revel with wine and song."

Just then a voice from a neighb'ring hill
Cried, "Rip Van Winkle!" and all was still
Then he looked above and he looked below,
And saw not a thing but a lonely crow.

"Ho, Rip Van Winkle!" the voice still cried,
And Wolfie skulked to his master's side.

Just then from a thicket a man came out—
His legs were short and his body stout,
He looked like a Dutchman in days of yore,
With buttons behind and buttons before;

And held a keg
with an iron grip,
And beckoned for help
to the gazing Rip.

Rip had his fears, but at last complied,
And bore the keg up the mountain side;
And now and then, when a thunder-peal
Made the mountain tremble, Rip would steal
A look at his guide, but never a word
From the lips of the queer old man was heard.

Up, up they clambered, until, at last,
The stranger halted. Rip quickly cast
A glance around, and as strange a crew

As ever a mortal man did view
Were playing at nine-pins; at every ball
'Twas fun to see how the pins would fall;
And they rolled and rolled, without speaking a word,
And this was the thunder Rip had heard.

Their hats looked odd, each with sugar-loaf crown,
And their eyes were small, and their beards hung down,
While their high-heeled shoes all had peaked tocs,
And their legs were covered with blood-red hose;
Their noses were long, like a porker's snout,
And they nodded and winked as they moved about.

They tapped the keg, and the liquor flowed,
And up to the brim of each flagon glowed;
And a queer old man made a sign to Rip,
As much as to say, "Will you take a nip?"

Nor did he linger or stop to think,
For Rip was thirsty and wanted a drink.
"I'll risk it," thought he; "it can be no sin,
And it smells like the best of Holland gin."

So he tipped his cup to a grim old chap,
And drained it; then, for a quiet nap,
He stretched himself on the mossy ground,
And soon was wrapped in a sleep profound.

At last he woke; 'twas a sunny morn,
And the strange old men of the glen were gone;
He saw the young birds flutter and hop,
And an eagle wheeled round the mountain-top;
Then he rubbed his eyes for another sight—
"Surely," said he, "I have slept all night."

He thought of the flagon and nine-pin game;
"Oh! what shall I say to my fiery dame?"
He, faintly faltered; "I know that she
Has a fearful lecture in store for me."
He took up his gun, and, strange to say,
The wood had rotted and worn away.
He raised to his feet, and his joints were sore;
Said he, "I must go to my home once more."

Then, with trembling step,
    he wandered down;
Amazed, he entered his
    native town.
The people looked with a
    wondering stare,
For Rip, alas! was a
    stranger there;
He tottered up to his
    cottage-door,
But his wife was dead and
    could scold no more;

And down at the tavern he sought in vain
For the chums he would never meet again;
He looked, as he passed, at a group of girls
For the laughing eye and the flaxen curls
Of the child he loved as he loved his life,
But she was a thrifty farmer's wife;
And when they met, and her hand he took,
She blushed and gave him a puzzled look;

But she knew her father and kissed his brow,
All covered with marks and wrinkles now;
For Rip Van Winkle was old and gray,
And twenty summers had passed away—

Yes, twenty winters of snow and frost
Had he in his mountain slumber lost;
Yet his love for stories was all the same,
And he often told of the nine-pin game.

But the age was getting a little fast—
The Revolution had come and passed,
And Young America, gathered about,
Received his tales with many a doubt,
Awhile he hobbled about the town;
Then, worn and weary, at last laid down,
For his locks were white and his limbs were sore
And RIP VAN WINKLE will wake no more.

A NOTE ABOUT WASHINGTON IRVING

"Rip Van Winkle," the story upon which this poem is based, was written by Washington Irving in London in 1820; it was included in a collection of satirical essays and stories entitled *The Sketch Book of Geoffrey Crayon, Gent*. At the time of its publication, Irving was already a literary legend at home and the first of his countrymen to have established a literary reputation abroad. *Geoffrey Crayon*, its author's masterpiece, was to solidify and extend that reputation on both sides of the Atlantic.

Irving was born in New York in 1783, of British immigrant parents. Intended from childhood for the legal profession, Irving amused himself in law school and later, after he had established his law practice, by writing satirical essays on New York society and theater which were eventually collected in several volumes. Among them was *A History of New York from the Beginning of the World to the End of the Dutch Dynasty* (1809), written under the pseudonym of Diedrich Knickerbocker. Originally intended as a satire on Dr. Samuel Mitchell's pretentious history of New York City, "Knickerbocker's" *History* has been called "the first great book of comic literature written by an American."

Upon the death of his father, Irving became a partner in the family business in Liverpool, England. The firm was doing badly financially, and even Irving's trip to England in 1815 and his personal efforts to keep the company solvent could not prevent its going bankrupt within a few years. At this point, Irving turned seriously to literature as a means of financial support. "Rip Van Winkle" was penned during this time.

From his prolific—and successful—writings, Irving achieved a certain degree of financial security, and soon after his return to the Untied States in 1824, he set out on a tour of the European continent. Irving eventually settled in Madrid, where he was appointed consul to the American embassy. In Madrid, he wrote *History of the Life and Voyages of Christopher Columbus* (1828); *The Conquest of Granada* (1829), a romantic narrative; and *The Alhambra: a series of tales and sketches of the Moors and Spaniards* (1832).

Irving returned home in 1832. After touring the western territories of the United States for the first time, he settled permanently in New York and established a retreat for himself—christened "Sunnyside"—near his old New York neighborhood on the Hudson.

Between 1842 and 1846, Irving served as the American ambassador to Spain. His duties left him little time for writing, so it was not until several years after his return from Madrid that his next work—*Life of Oliver Goldsmith, with Selections from his Writings* (1849)—appeared in print. Irving continued publishing works until his death, at Sunnyside on November 28, 1859.

NANCY GOLDBERG